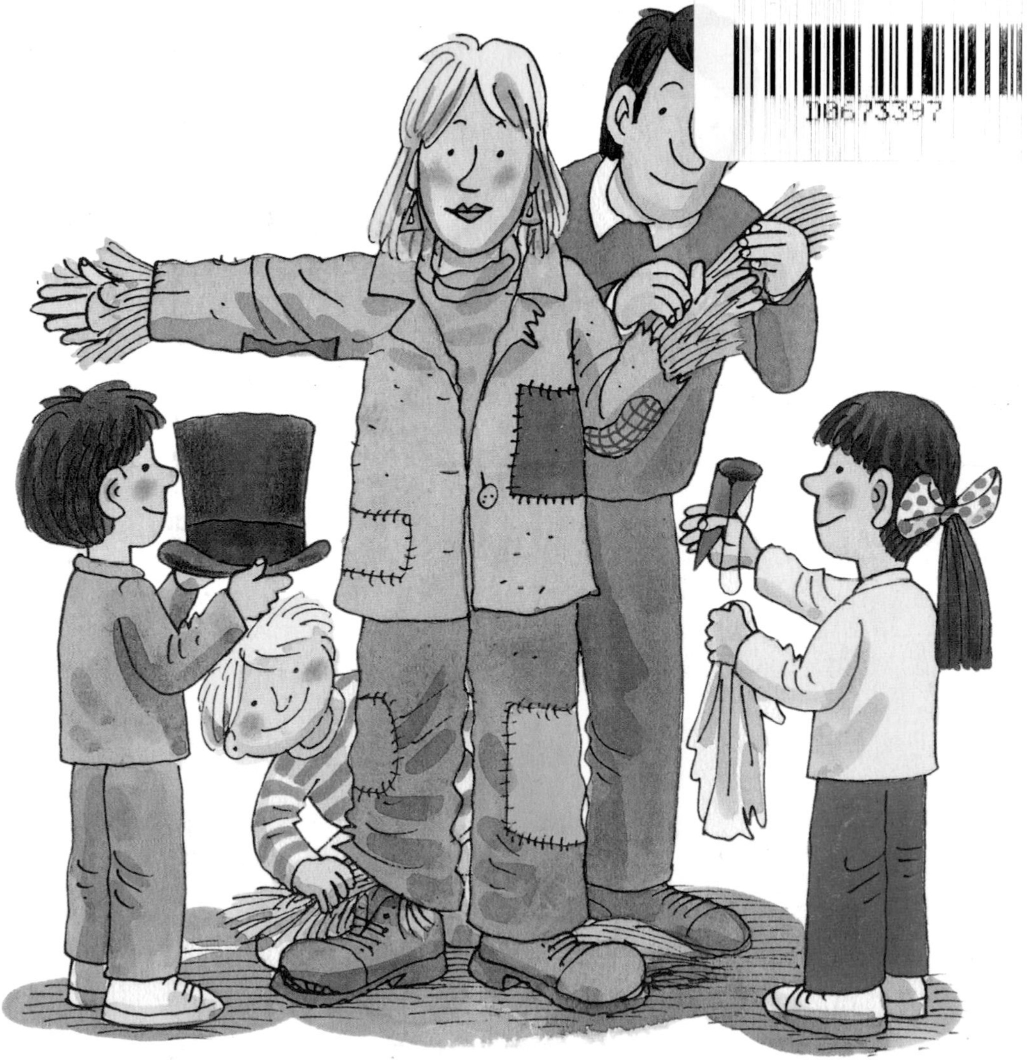

Mum was a scarecrow.

Biff was a pirate.

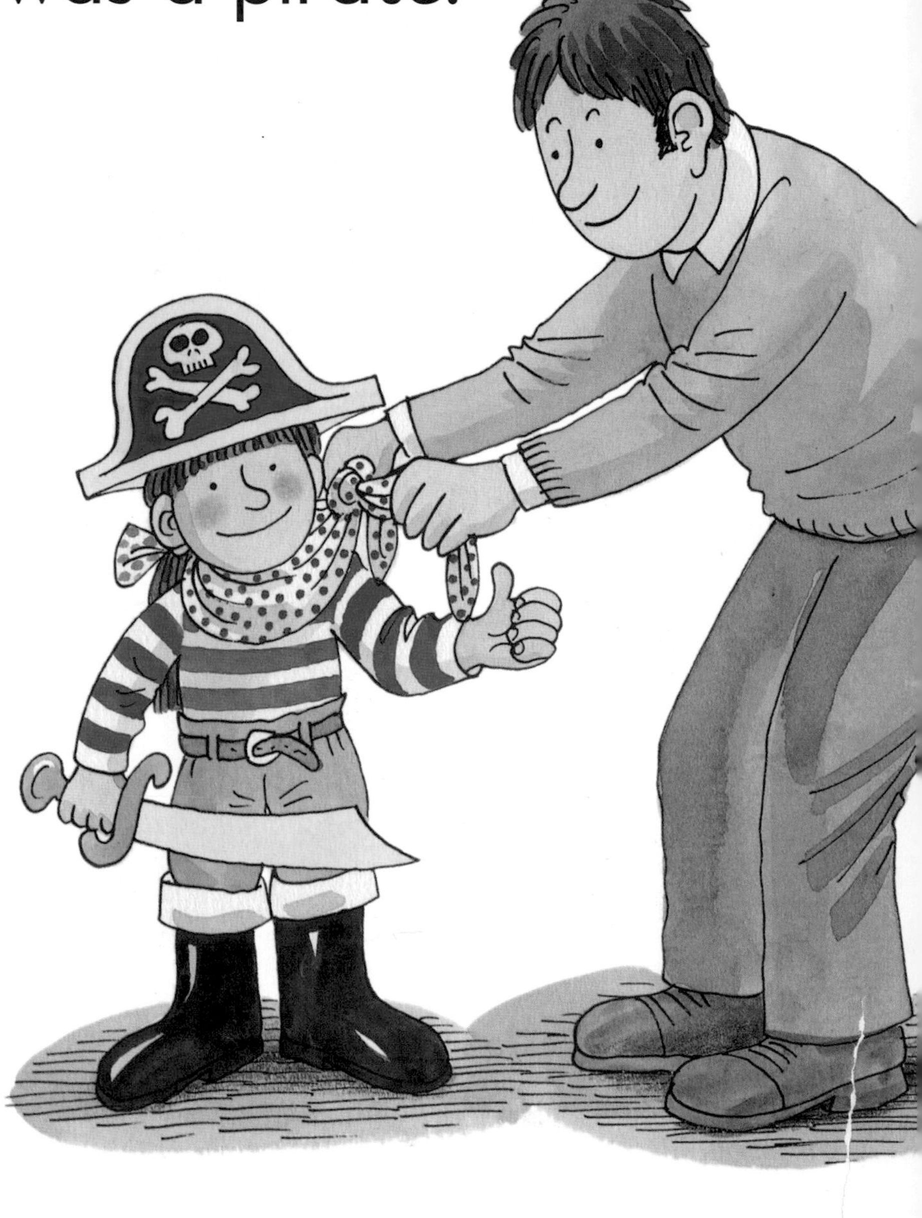

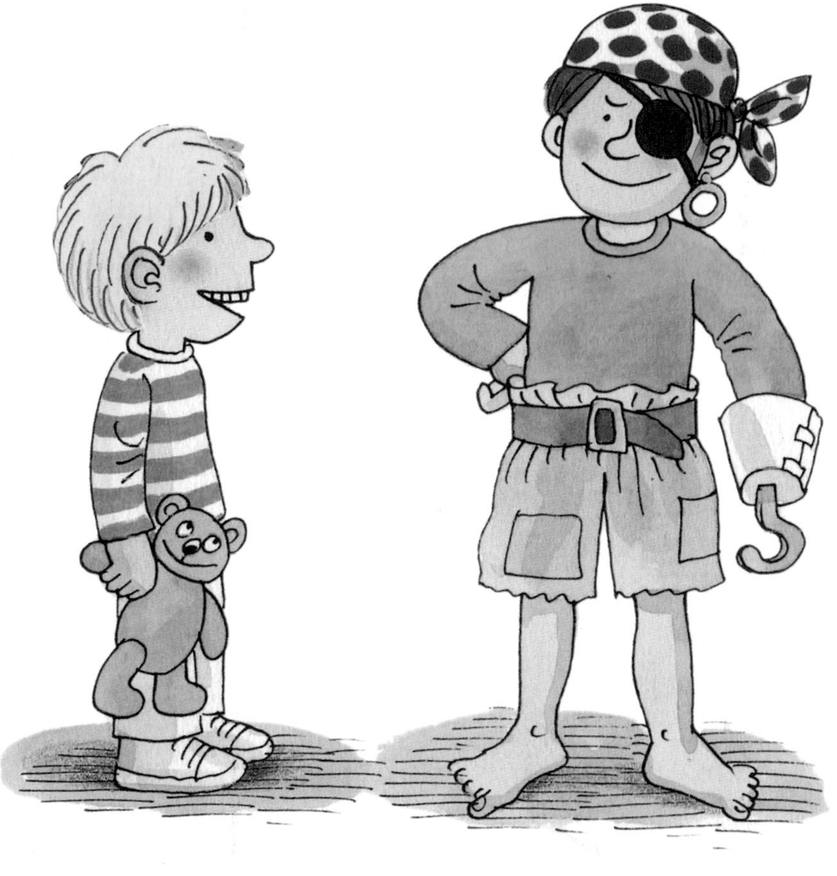

Chip was a pirate.

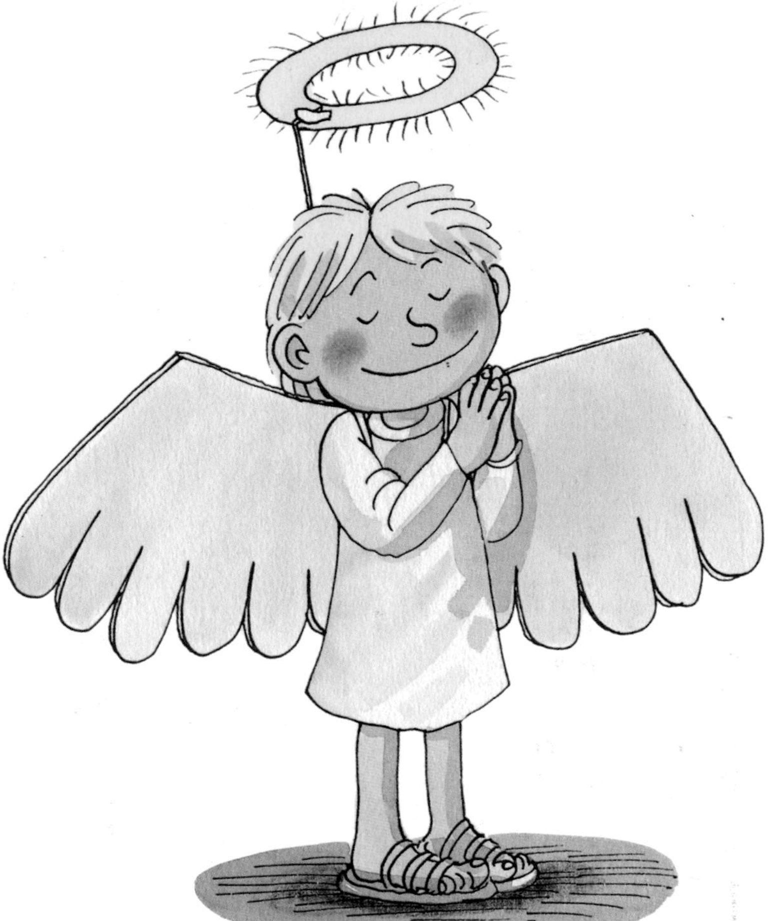

Kipper was an angel.

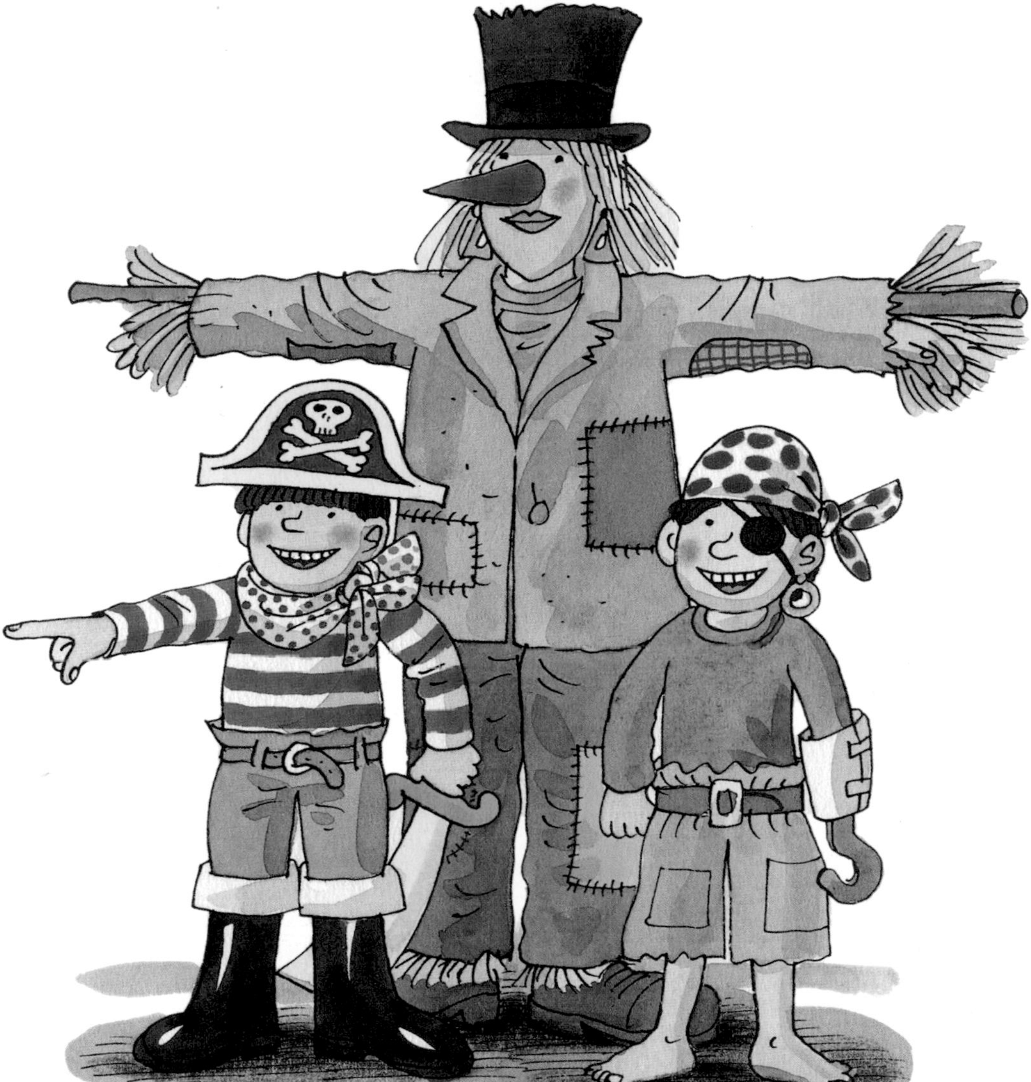

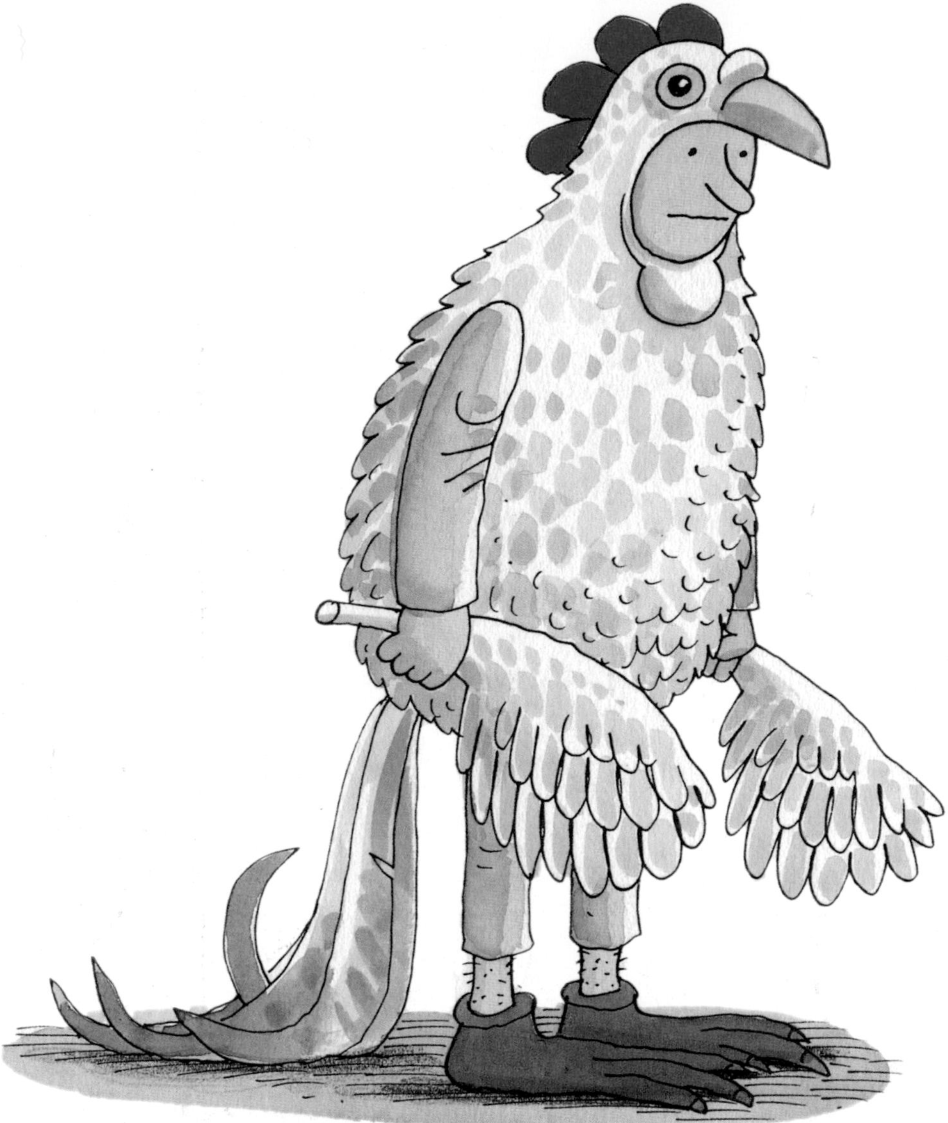

Dad was a chicken.

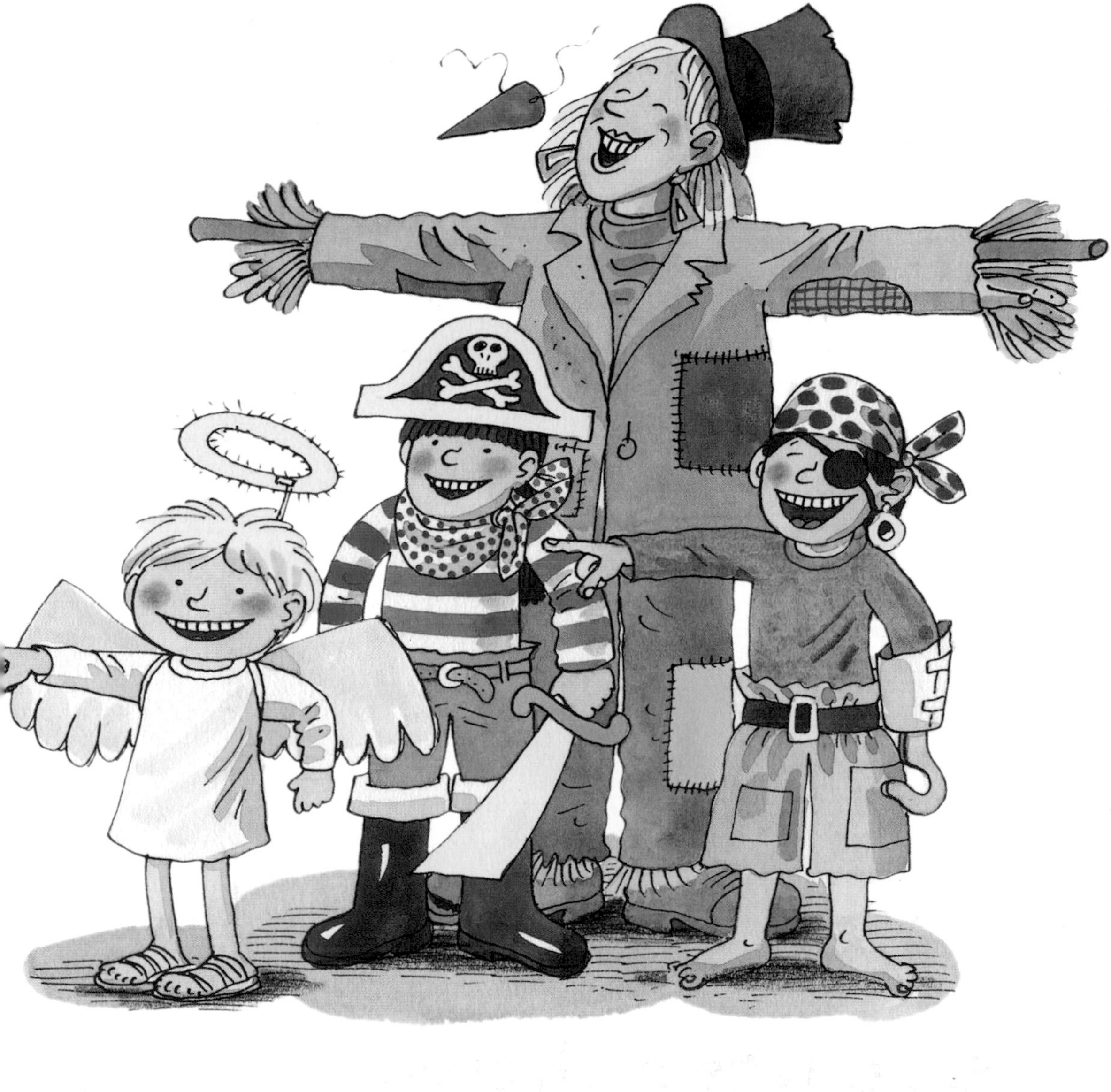

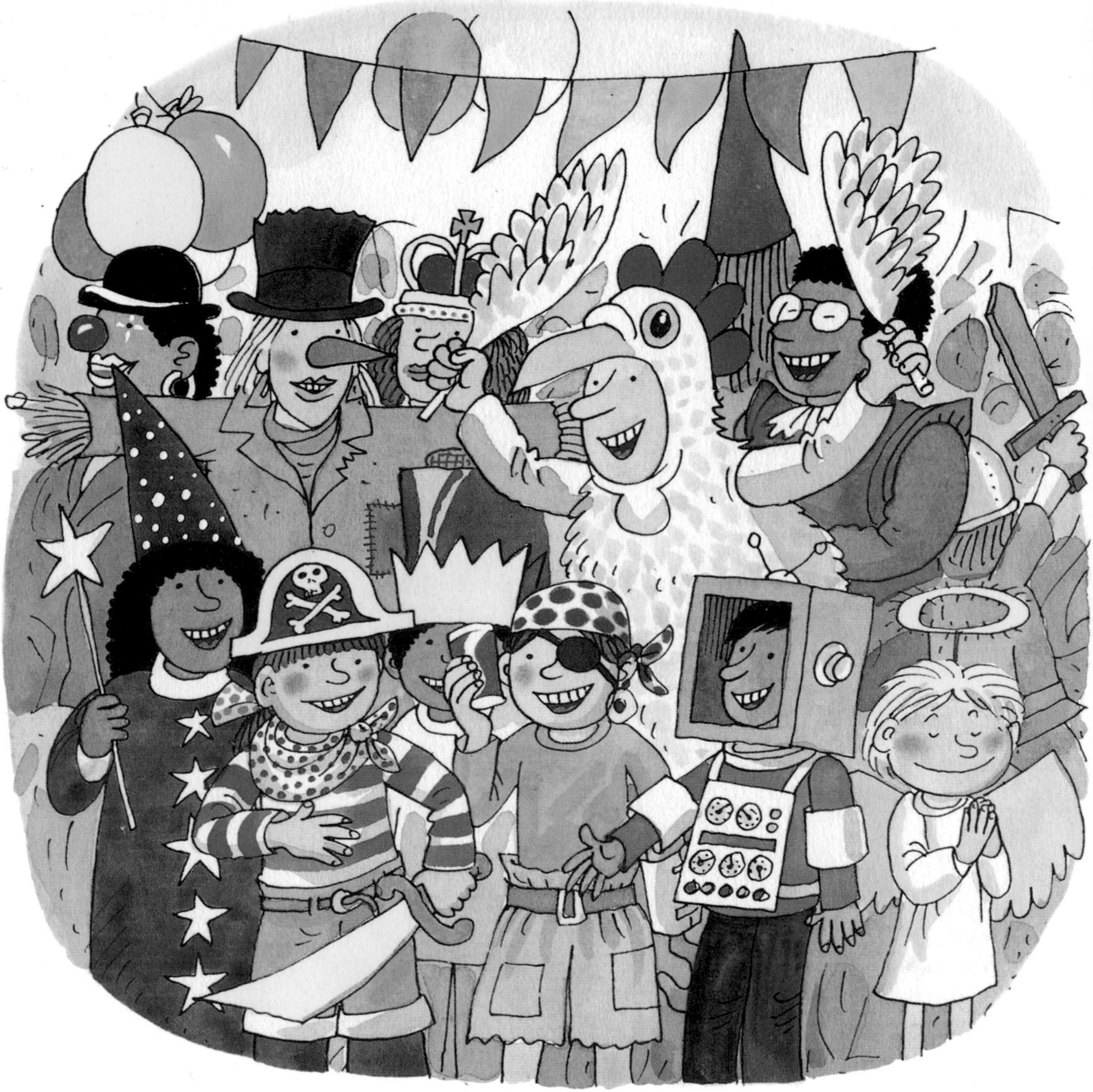

Everyone was happy.